Desert Critter Friends

Jumping Jokers

Mona Gansberg Hodgson

Illustrated by Chris Sharp

CPH
SAINT LOUIS

Dedicated with much love to my sisters—Cindy Hilton, Tammy Haydon, and Linda Smith. I'm so glad we're sisters and friends.

Desert Critter Friends Series

Friendly Differences

Thorny Treasures

Sour Snacks

Smelly Tales

Clubhouse Surprises

Desert Detectives

Campout Capers

Jumping Jokers

Scripture quotations are taken from the HOLY BIBLE, NEW INTERNATIONAL VERSION®. NIV®. Copyright © 1973, 1978, 1984 by International Bible Society. Used by permission of Zondervan Publishing House. All rights reserved.

Text copyright © 1999 Mona Gansberg Hodgson

Published by Concordia Publishing House
3558 S. Jefferson Avenue, St. Louis, MO 63118-3968
Manufactured in the United States of America

Library of Congress Cataloging-in-Publication Data

Hodgson, Mona Gansberg, 1954–
    Jumping jokers / Mona Gansberg Hodgson ; illustrated by Chris Sharp.
       p.   cm. — (Desert Critter Friends ; bk 7)
    Summary: When Jamal the jackrabbit inadvertently leads a coyote to Toby and Wanda's burrow, it is difficult for Toby to forgive Jamal for forcing them to move to a new home. Additional text discusses how God wants us to be forgiving.
    ISBN 0-570-05481-8
    [1. Forgiveness—Fiction. 2. Rabbits—Fiction. 3. Desert animals—Fiction. 4. Christian life—Fiction.] I. Sharp, Chris, 1954- ill. II. Title. III. Series: Hodgson, Mona Gansberg, 1954– Desert Critter Friends ; bk. 7.
PZ7.H6649Ju   1999
[E]—dc21   98-54265

1 2 3 4 5 6 7 8 9 10   08 07 06 05 04 03 02 01 00 99

Toby, the cottontail, hopped toward his home. He leaped over lizards. He sprang over spiders. Just a few hops away from home, Toby stopped. His nose wiggled as he sniffed the air. *SNIFF! SNIFF!* Things didn't smell right.

Toby looked to the left. He looked to the right. He didn't see anyone. But he did see coyote footprints! A coyote had come to Toby's house.

Creeping over to his burrow, Toby saw piles of dirt where the coyote had dug. He hopped all around. Where was his sister, Wanda?

Toby heard someone coming. Maybe it was Wanda. But what if it was the coyote? Toby darted under a bush.

ZOOM! Bert, the roadrunner, zoomed up to Toby's burrow.

Toby hopped over to Bert.
"Have you seen Wanda?"

Bert stared at the piles of dirt.
He pulled on his cap. "What
happened here?"

"A coyote came to visit," Toby said. "I'm okay, but I don't know where Wanda is."

"I haven't seen her. She probably just went for a morning hop."

"I hope you're right," Toby twitched his nose.

"Let's go find Wanda." Bert took off. *ZOOM!* Toby hopped after him. *SCREECH!* Bert stopped in front of Nadine, the javelina (*have-a-lena*). She was back from her vacation. Toby hopped up to her.

"Hi, there, Toby," Nadine said. "Bert just told me about seeing coyote footprints by your burrow."

"Yes. We'll have to move again." Toby frowned. "We're looking for Wanda. Have you seen her?"

"No, but I'm going to meet Rosie and Myra at the clubhouse for lunch today. Wanda might be there too." Nadine looked up at the sun. "Oh dear, I'm running late! I've got to go."

"We'll see you at the clubhouse then," Bert said. *ZOOM!* Bert zoomed away.

Toby hopped after the roadrunner. Nadine moseyed down the
path behind them.

All of a sudden someone yelled,
"BOO!" Toby saw his friend Jamal,

the jackrabbit, jump out of the
bushes in front of them.

Bert stopped. *SCREECH!*

Toby was hopping too fast to
stop. He hopped right into Bert. Bert
and Toby tumbled into the weeds.

"HO! HO! HO!" Jamal laughed. He thumped his two huge back feet. "Got you guys good, didn't I?"

Toby wasn't laughing. He jumped to his feet and frowned at Jamal.

"Looks like you're in a bad mood!" Jamal tugged on his bandana.

"I have things to do." Toby stomped his feet. "And I don't have time for games!"

Bert pulled his cap back on his head. "Have you seen Wanda?"

"You're looking for Wanda?" Jamal asked.

Bert loosened the straps on his backpack. "A coyote came to visit the burrow while Toby was gone this morning."

Jamal gulped. "Oh, no! I didn't even think about your burrow."

Toby's ears stood up straight. "What are you talking about?"

"I was ..." Jamal paused and gulped again. "I was teasing the coyote this morning." His big ears hung low. "I didn't mean for him to find your burrow."

"Well, he did!" Toby stomped again.

Nadine strolled up to them. "What's going on?"

Bert looked at Jamal. "Sounds like you played a dangerous game."

"You helped the coyote find
Toby and Wanda's home?" Nadine
grunted at Jamal.

"I'm sorry," said Jamal. "I
didn't mean ..."

Toby interrupted Jamal.
"Because of you, we have to find a
new place for our burrow." He
stomped again.

"I'm sorry, Toby." Jamal's eyes
filled with tears. "I didn't mean for
any of this to happen. Please
forgive me."

"I can't forgive you!" Toby
shouted. "I have to go find
Wanda!" Toby hopped away.
Nadine followed him.

Toby hopped to the Desert
Critter Clubhouse. He was out of
breath. *PUFF! PUFF!* He heard
Wanda's voice inside and jumped
through the door.

Myra, the quail, was surprised. She dumped her bowl of seeds right on Toby's head.

Wanda giggled at the seeds in her brother's ears. Jill and Rosie giggled, too.

"I'm so glad you are safe!" Toby hugged Wanda. Myra scooped up seeds.

Nadine strolled into the clubhouse. "Hi! I'm glad you're here, Wanda. Toby was looking for you."

Wanda twitched her nose and stared at Toby. "What's going on?"

"It's a long story." Toby sighed. "Jamal was teasing a coyote. The coyote found our burrow and—"

Wanda's ears stood up straight. "We have to move again?"

"Don't worry," Toby said.

"*ACHOO!*" Rosie sneezed. "After lunch we will help you find a new place."

"This was to be a girls' lunch," Jill told Toby. "But I guess you can join us."

"Better make room for another boy," Nadine mumbled. "Bert is on his way."

Jill pulled two more plates and cups from the shelf. Rosie put a plate of prickly pear sandwiches on the table. Wanda poured cactus juice into the cups. Myra put the bowl of seeds on the table.

ZOOM! Bert zoomed into the clubhouse. "Glad you're here, Wanda. Looks like I'm just in time for lunch."

After lunch the critters went to Toby and Wanda's old burrow. Jamal was already there.

Toby watched Jamal gather some of their things in his bandana.

Jamal saw the desert critters. He hopped over to Wanda. "Wanda, I

never meant for the coyote to find your burrow. Will you please forgive me?"

"I don't like having to move again. But, yes, I forgive you." Wanda smiled at Jamal.

Toby wondered how Wanda could forgive Jamal.

Jamal hugged Wanda. Then he hopped to Toby. "I found a great place for your new burrow."

Toby stomped at Jamal.

Wanda frowned at Toby. "I think we should see what Jamal found."

ZOOM! Bert packed some of the rabbits' things in his backpack. "You can't stay mad at Jamal," he told Toby. "He's your friend!"

"*ACHOO!*" Rosie pulled a tissue out of her tennis shoe. "And friends forgive one another."

Toby stared at the ground. He looked at the jackrabbit. "Okay, take us to see this place you found."

Jamal stopped near an acacia
tree. "Here it is!"

Bert took off his backpack and
zoomed around. Toby looked
around. This was a great place for
a new burrow. But he wouldn't *need*
a new home if it weren't for that
jumping joker Jamal.

Wanda pointed to the acacia tree. "We can dig our hole right there under that tree. It's shady. And I can use that low branch for a clothesline."

ZOOM! Bert zoomed over to the rabbits. He pointed toward a gully. "There's water right over there."

"What a great place for your new burrow!" Jill said.

Toby started digging. *DIG! DIG! DIG!* Dirt sprayed out behind Toby. Dirt sprayed right where Rosie kneeled to tie her shoe.

"*Achoo!*"

"*ACHOO! ACHOO! ACHOO!*"
Rosie tried to move, but she was
sneezing too hard to get up.
"*ACHOO! ACHOO! ACHOO! ACHOO!
ACHOO! ACHOO!*" Rosie was
sneezing so hard she fell over.

All the critters hurried over to
Rosie.

Except Toby. *DIG! DIG! DIG!* All Toby could think about was what Jamal had done.

"STOP! TOBY!" Wanda shouted and jumped up and down. "STOP!"

"*ACHOO! ACHOO! ACHOO!*"

Toby stopped digging. He turned around. "Rosie! I didn't see you!"

"*ACHOO! ACHOO! ACHOO!*"

34

"Now you've really stirred up her allergies." Nadine grunted at Toby.

"*ACHOO! ACHOO! ACHOO!*"

"I'm sorry," Toby said. "I didn't mean to make you sneeze."

"*ACHOO! ACHOO! ACHOO!*"

Wanda hopped up and down. "We have to do something!"

Toby looked at Bert. "What can we do?"

"ACHOO! ACHOO! ACHOO!"

Bert grabbed his backpack. He pulled out a rag and his water bottle. Then he poured water on the rag. He put the wet rag up to Rosie's nose. "Try to take a deep breath," he told her.

Rosie breathed through the rag.

"Do it again," Bert said.

Rosie took another breath of mist. Then another one. She wasn't sneezing anymore.

Toby sighed. "I'm so sorry, Rosie. I didn't mean to—"

"It's okay, Toby. I forgive you." Rosie smiled at Toby.

Toby began to think. How could Rosie forgive him? He had kicked dirt all over her and even made her sick. Toby knew what to do.

Toby hopped over to Jamal. "Rosie was right. Friends forgive each other. I forgive you, Jamal."

Jamal thumped his huge back feet. He gave Toby a big hug.

"I even have a joke for you," Toby said.

Toby cleared his throat. "What has big ears but doesn't always hear? *Me!*"

"*Ha! Ha! Ho!*" Toby laughed.

"*Ho! Ho! Ho!*" Jamal laughed.

All the friends laughed.

God loves you so much that He sent His Son, Jesus, to die for you. Jesus died to pay for your sins. Now you can be forgiven. Jesus will help you forgive others.

Hi, kids!

Be kind and compassionate to one another, forgiving each other, just as in Christ God forgave you. Ephesians 4:32

Here's a list of the desert critter friends. Fill in the names of the critters to finish the crossword puzzle.

COTTONTAIL RABBITS

COYOTE

GROUND SQUIRREL

JACKRABBIT

JAVELINA

QUAIL

ROADRUNNER

SKUNK

For Parents and Teachers:

Toby wanted to place blame and make someone pay for his suffering whether it was appropriate or not. Sound like any kids (or adults) you know?

While anger is a valid emotion, it carries the potential for destruction. Unresolved anger can harm us emotionally, physically, and spiritually when we refuse to forgive others. It can destroy friendships and family relationships. In Matthew 6:15 Jesus says that our motivation for forgiving others comes from the forgiveness that His Father showers on us. An unforgiving spirit affects our fellowship with others and our fellowship with God.

Jamal didn't mean for his games with the coyote to cause trouble for Toby and Wanda. Toby didn't mean to kick dirt into Rosie's face and make her sick. Neither critter considered the consequences of his actions.

Help your children understand that their actions have consequences, both positive and negative. God helps us take responsibility for our actions and our emotions. He helps us deal with our anger in constructive ways. He calls us to accept the forgiveness won by His Son. He helps us to forgive others.

Here are some questions and activities you can use as discussion starters to help your children understand these concepts.

Discussion Starters

1. Why was Toby mad at Jamal?

2. Has anyone ever done anything that made you mad? What did you do?

3. How did Jamal get himself into trouble? Have you ever caused trouble without thinking about what would happen?

4. How did Jamal feel about what he had done?

5. What can you do when you find out that you have hurt someone—accidentally or on purpose? How will God help you?

6. What does God's Word tell us about forgiveness?

Pray together. Thank God for sending His Son to be your Savior. Thank God for forgiving your sins. Ask Him to help you forgive others.

God will help you forgive others. Use these lines to tell me what you will do the next time someone makes you mad.